I AM EXCEPTIONAL

I AM
EXCEPTIONAL

Written by: Elaine Bender
Illustrated by: Ty Schafrath

XULON PRESS

Xulon Press
2301 Lucien Way #415
Maitland, FL 32751
407.339.4217
www.xulonpress.com

Unless otherwise indicated, Scripture quotations taken from the Holy
Bible, New International Version (NIV). Copyright © 1973, 1978, 1984,
2011 by Biblica, Inc.™. Used by permission. All rights reserved.

Scripture quotations taken from the Holy Bible, New Living Translation
(NLT). Copyright ©1996, 2004, 2007 by Tyndale House Foundation. Used
by permission of Tyndale House Publishers, Inc.

Scripture quotations taken from The Message (MSG). Copyright © 1993,
1994, 1995, 1996, 2000, 2001, 2002. Used by permission of NavPress
Publishing Group. Used by permission. All rights reserved.

Printed in the United States of America.

ISBN-13: 978-1-54564-600-7

Purposed **L**oved

I am exceptional.
I was made with a PLAN.

I was created by the
Great I AM.

"For I know the plans I have for you," says the LORD. "They are plans for good and not for disaster, to give you a future and a hope."
Jeremiah 29:11 (NLT)

My family calls me:

Birth
Certificate

Name

Date

But you are the ones chosen by God, chosen for the high calling
of priestly work, chosen to be a holy people, God's instruments

But my God up above calls me:

Healthy

Chosen

Prosperous

and...

Loved

to do his work and speak out for him...

1 Peter 2:9-10 (MSG)

9

My ears do not quite hear like most others,

but the Shepherd's voice I hear like my brothers.

My sheep listen to my voice; I know them, and they follow me.

John 10:27 (NIV)

Glasses I have
to help me see,

but I never lose sight
of His Word for me.

My son, pay attention to what I say; turn your ear to my words. Do not
let them out of your sight, keep them within your heart; for they are
life to those who find them and health to one's whole body.

Proverbs 4:20-22 (NIV)

When I talk, it may
not be clear,

but my faith has the power to make things appear.

Then Jesus told them, "I tell you the truth, if you have faith and don't doubt, you can do things like this and much more. You can even say to this mountain, 'May you be lifted up and thrown into the sea,' and it will happen."

Matthew 21:21 (NLT)

I may not walk just the same,

but the narrow path
is always my aim.

But small is the gate and narrow the road that leads to life, and only
a few find it.

Matthew 7:14 (NIV)

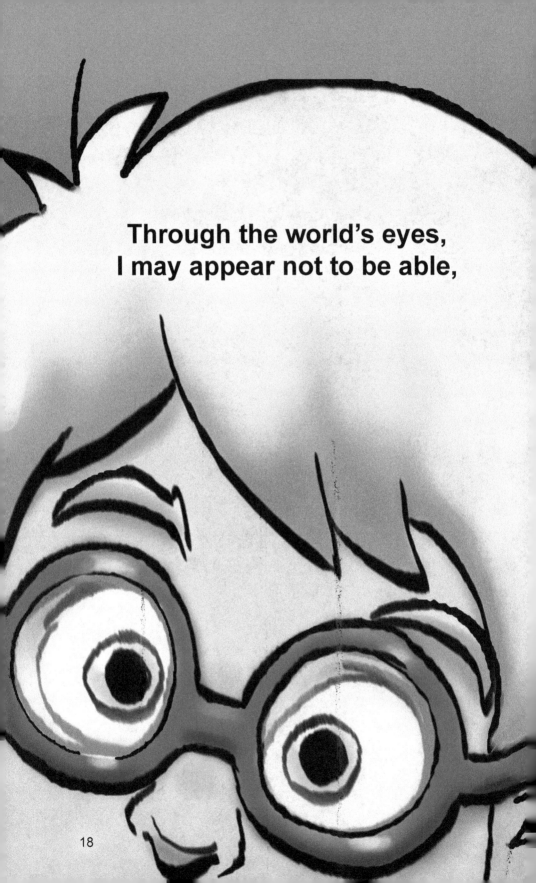

Through the world's eyes,
I may appear not to be able,

18

but God says:

Jesus looked at them and said, "With man this is impossible, but with God all things are possible."

Matthew 19:26 (NIV)

Through my weakness,
God shows forth His grace.

He uses His power
to take my place.

Each time he said, "My grace is all you need. My power works best in weakness." So now I am glad to boast about my weaknesses, so that the power of Christ can work through me.

2 Corinthians 12:9 (NLT)

We have one life here,
and I am here,
just like you,

to be a light to the world
and let them know
what is true.

You are the light of the world—like a city on a hilltop that cannot be hidden.

Matthew 5:14 (NLT)

24

**Our gifts and talents
might not be alike,**

**but all are needed
despite what it looks like.**

God has given each of you a gift from his great variety of spiritual gifts. Use them well to serve one another.

1 Peter 4:10 (NLT)

**Serving together
with passion we will give,**

and show those around us how we should live.

All Scripture is inspired by God and is useful to teach us what is true and to make us realize what is wrong in our lives. It corrects us when we are wrong and teaches us to do what is right.

2 Timothy 3:16 (NLT)

Mountains will move
just as we expect.

Miracles will happen
that no one can object.

He does great things too marvelous to understand. He performs
countless miracles.

Job 5:9 (NLT)

Our world needs to see the
change in our heart,

so let's work together
and do our part.

A servant of the Lord must not quarrel but must be kind to everyone,
be able to teach, and be patient with difficult people.

2 Timothy 2:24 (NLT)

**And praise our God
for this life that we live and
His amazing son,
Jesus,
for serving as He did!**

Let all that I am praise the LORD; with my whole heart, I will praise
his holy name.

Psalm 103:1 (NLT)

CPSIA information can be obtained
at www.ICGtesting.com
Printed in the USA
BVHW011204061119
563079BV00004B/27/P